DARK LABYRINTH

Laura Shenton

DARK LABYRINTH

Laura Shenton

Iridescent Toad Publishing

Iridescent Toad Publishing.

Cover by Kuro Ishi Arts.

First edition. ISBN 978-1-913779-24-5

Chapter One

Maya's iridescent wings caught the afternoon light as she flitted between the forest floor and the lower branches of the ancient oaks, their gnarled bark etched with centuries of growth. Her delicate fae form cast dancing shadows across the moss-covered ground as she worked, her movements graceful and purposeful. The intricately woven basket at her hip – crafted from flexible young willow stems, just as her grandmother had taught her – grew heavy with the day's findings. Wild berries that glistened like polished jewels nestled against nuts that had fallen prematurely in the unrelenting summer heat, and in the corners rested the occasional mushroom, chosen with the same careful, methodical precision her grandmother had instilled in her.

The forest had always been kind to Maya. It provided not just sustenance, but joy, comfort, and the only home she had ever known or desired. The interlacing canopy overhead, a patchwork of emerald and jade, sheltered her from harsh weather and the prying eyes of the world beyond. The gentle rustling of leaves spoke a language she had grown to understand over years of attentive listening – warnings of approaching storms carried on changing air pressures, whispers of seasonal changes marked by subtle shifts in colour and scent, lullabies in the evening breeze that caressed her pointed ears as she drifted to sleep each night.

"Almost done," she murmured to herself, her voice barely disturbing the tranquil forest air as she examined a cluster of plump blackberries.

The juice-swollen fruits hung heavy on thorny branches. She selected only the ripest among them, her slender fingers moving with practiced precision, careful not to take too many from any single bush. Balance was everything in the forest – a delicate dance of giving and taking that sustained all life within its boundaries. Her grandmother had taught her that sacred principle before Maya could even fly properly, back when her young wings were still damp and clumsy with youth.

At nineteen, Maya was considered young among the forest fae, whose lifespans stretched across centuries like the roots of the ancient trees they called home, yet she had already established herself as one of the most reliable gatherers in their small, close-knit community. Her mother often boasted of her keen eye and gentle touch with growing things during evening gatherings, though Maya brushed off such praise with embarrassed smiles and downcast eyes that sparkled despite her modesty.

"Maya has a strong instinct for the forest," her grandmother would say, her ancient eyes crinkling at the corners, her papery skin folding into familiar patterns of affection and pride. "The trees whisper their secrets to her when they think no one is listening."

What nobody said – though everyone knew, in that way small communities hold collective knowledge – was that Maya's dedication to gathering stemmed partly from necessity. Her father had vanished when she was still a child, his wings catching the dawn light one morning before he flew off on a routine trading expedition, never to return. He was one of many fae who had simply disappeared over the years, leaving behind unanswered questions and hollow spaces in the hearts of those who remained. The elders spoke of cycles and natural patterns with solemn faces and knowing nods, but Maya's mother grew quiet whenever the subject arose, her normally melodious voice falling silent, her eyes distant with memories she refused to share. So Maya gathered, ensuring their small family never went without, her young shoulders bearing a weight invisible to those who didn't look closely enough.

As the day progressed towards evening, golden light slanting through the trees at increasingly steep angles, Maya decided to take a final sweep through her favourite clearing before heading home. The soft carpet of clover felt cool and soothing beneath her bare feet as she landed, giving her wings – now slightly tired from hours of continuous use – a well-deserved rest. Here, wildflowers grew in abundance, their faces turned towards the patches of sunlight that broke through the canopy. The ground was often dotted with small creatures going about their business in the safety of the open space, their tiny lives intersecting briefly with her own.

That's when she spotted the field mouse – a tiny brown creature with alert ears that swivelled like miniature sentinels and bright, beady eyes that reflected the waning daylight. It was nibbling on a seed plucked from the tall grasses at the clearing's edge, its whiskers twitching with each tiny but eager bite.

Maya smiled, her face softening with genuine affection. She had always had a soft spot for the forest's smallest denizens, finding beauty in their humble existence where others might overlook them entirely. Setting her basket aside on a patch of particularly lush clover, she knelt, her movements slow and considered to avoid startling her diminutive companion.

"Hello there, little one," she cooed, keeping her voice soft and melodic, the natural music of fae speech gentled even further. "Busy day? Found anything interesting among the grasses?"

The mouse paused in its feast, its nose quivering rapidly as it assessed Maya. Its tiny chest rose and fell with quick breaths, ready to flee at the first sign of danger. Most creatures in the forest were accustomed to the presence of fae, knowing them to be harmless, even helpful at times when drought or disease threatened. After a moment of careful consideration, the mouse returned to its seed, though it kept one bright eye trained on her, unwilling to completely lower its guard.

Maya reached into her basket and extracted a single, perfect blackberry, its surface still cool from the shade where she'd found it. With delicate fingers, she separated one of the dark drupelets, its skin breaking slightly to release a drop of sweet-tart juice that stained her fingertip purple. She placed it ceremoniously on a broad leaf near the mouse, arranging it like an offering on a miniature altar. Then she waited, perfectly still save for the slight, involuntary flutter of her wings – an unconscious habit when she was pleased or excited that had persisted from childhood.

The mouse's nose twitched more intensely as the sweet scent reached it, overpowering the earthy smells of soil and vegetation. Cautiously, whiskers forward and body tense, it approached the offering. With lightning-fast speed born of survival instinct, it snatched up the morsel and scurried back a safe distance before consuming its prize, its tiny paws holding the fruit as it nibbled with obvious delight.

Maya laughed, a sound like small silver bells in the forest quiet, the noise startling a nearby cricket into momentary silence.

"Would you like another?" she asked, already separating a second piece with gentle fingers. "I have plenty to share, and you're certainly appreciative."

The game continued for several minutes – Maya offering tiny morsels, each placed a bit closer to herself than the last, the mouse growing bolder with each approach. Soon, its hunger and growing trust overcoming caution, it was eating directly from her palm, its tiny paws gripping her finger for balance, its whiskers tickling her skin with feather-light touches.

"You're braver than you look," Maya told it, watching as it finished the last of the berry, its muzzle stained with purple juice that it would spend hours grooming away. "Most of your kind would never venture so close to someone as large as me. Perhaps I should call you Valour. It suits you, I think."

The newly christened Valour seemed to approve of its name, its whiskers twitching as it cleaned its paws fastidiously, drawing them over its face in habitual motions. Then, without warning, as if responding to a signal Maya couldn't perceive, it darted away, streaking across the clearing towards the massive trunk of an ancient oak that Maya had never paid particular attention to before. This tree stood slightly apart from its brethren, its bark darker, its roots more pronounced as they plunged into the earth.

"Wait!" Maya called, rising to her feet in surprise, leaves and bits of clover clinging to her garments. Something about the mouse's sudden departure struck her as odd, almost alarmed. It had seemed so content just moments before, its movements relaxed and unhurried.

She watched, puzzled, as Valour disappeared into a small opening at the base of the tree –

a dark gap between two enormous roots that twisted down into the earth like serpents. Maya might have dismissed it as a simple mouse hole, a cosy burrow where the creature made its home, but something cold settled in her stomach, a premonition that prickled along her spine and made her wings stiffen. The opening seemed too perfect, too deliberately shaped to be the work of nature alone.

Maya knew she should turn away, gather her basket, and head home through the lengthening shadows. Her mother and grandmother would be expecting her, perhaps already glancing anxiously towards the forest path, and the sun was already beginning to dip behind the tallest trees, painting the sky in watercolour hues of orange and pink. Yet she remained rooted in place, staring at the dark opening as if mesmerised. What if the mouse was in danger? What if it had been frightened by something Maya hadn't noticed – a predator lurking unseen in the tall grasses or the shadows between trees?

"This is silly," she whispered to herself, even as she took a step forward, drawn by curiosity and concern in equal measure. "It's just a hole in a tree. A perfectly normal burrow where that mouse probably stores seeds for winter."

But the forest had taught Maya to trust her instincts, the quiet inner voice that sometimes warned of unseen dangers or guided her to particularly abundant berry patches. And something about that dark space called to her. Not in invitation, but in warning – a siren song that her better judgment urged her to resist even as her feet carried her closer.

She took another step forward, then another, her wings lifting her slightly so her approach was silent across the clover. The opening in the tree seemed to grow darker the closer she got, as though it was drinking in the surrounding light, a void that refused illumination.

"Valour?" she called softly, kneeling before the gap, her wings folded tightly against her back as she leaned forward. "Are you all right in there? Is something wrong?"

No response came, not even the scrabbling of tiny paws that would indicate the mouse was simply going about its business in its home. The silence was absolute, as if the very air around the opening absorbed sound.

Maya bit her lip, a nervous habit from childhood, indecision warring within her. Her rational mind presented reasonable explanations: The mouse might be perfectly fine, just shy or startled by her call. It might have simply returned to its nest after enjoying an unexpected feast, now curled contentedly among stored seeds and soft bedding materials. But what if it wasn't fine? What if it had sensed a predator and fled, only to find itself trapped? What if it was injured, bleeding from some unseen wound in the darkness where no one would find it?

"I'll just take a quick look," she reasoned, one hand absently fidgeting with the hem of her leaf-woven tunic. "Just to be sure it's safe, then I'll go straight home. Mother need never know I was delayed."

The opening was larger than it had first appeared – certainly big enough for a fae of Maya's slender build to enter, though she would need to duck her head and fold her wings tightly against her spine. A cool draft emerged from within, carrying a scent Maya couldn't identify, earthy yet metallic, like freshly turned soil laced with something else – something strange and unsettling that she had never encountered before.

Fear fluttered in her chest, beating against her ribs like a trapped bird seeking freedom. Yet concern for the little creature overrode her apprehension, drowning out the warning bells chiming in her mind. Maya had never turned her back on any being in need, no matter how small or seemingly insignificant. It was a quality her grandmother called both her greatest strength and her most dangerous weakness.

Taking a deep breath to steady herself, drawing the familiar forest air deep into her lungs, she spread her wings slightly for balance and darted into the darkness. She told herself firmly that she would only go far enough to ensure Valour was safe before retreating to the familiar comfort of the forest, where fresh air and gentle breezes awaited.

The moment she passed the threshold, Maya knew she had made a terrible mistake. The darkness was not the gentle, dappled shade of the forest floor but an absolute absence of light that seemed to press against her skin like a physical weight, suffocating in its intensity. The air was stale and cold, lacking the vibrant life-scent of her world above, devoid of the mingled aromas of flowers, leaves, and healthy soil that she had breathed her entire life.

Before she could turn back, before her eyes could even begin to adjust to the gloom, Maya felt strong hands grasp her arms from either side, fingers digging painfully into her flesh. A gasp escaped her lips as she was lifted off her feet, her wings trapped painfully against her back, the delicate membranes folded at unnatural angles that sent sharp spikes of pain through her shoulder blades.

"She's ours now," a deep voice growled near her ear, the words accompanied by breath that smelt of rot and something sickly-sweet that assaulted her nostrils.

"A fine little trespasser indeed," replied another, this one higher pitched but no less menacing, a hint of cruel amusement threading through the words. "The mouse worked perfectly."

Maya screamed, though she knew with sinking certainty that no one would hear her this far from the forest path. A large hand clamped over her mouth, rough skin pressing against her lips, muffling her cries. She kicked and thrashed with all her strength, her wings straining uselessly against their grip, but it was like fighting against stone. Their strength was overwhelming, their hold confident and efficient. It was as if they had done this many times before. As if they had been waiting specifically for her, a trap set with patience and precision.

As they began to drag her deeper into the darkness, away from the world she knew, Maya's last glimpse of the outside world – a small circle of green and gold light framed by root and earth – disappeared around a bend in the tunnel. And with it went all hope of an easy escape, leaving her at the mercy of her captors and the terrifying realisation that the disappearances her people had whispered about for years were neither accidents nor natural cycles, but something far more sinister.

Chapter Two

The journey through the darkness seemed endless, a nightmare from which Maya couldn't awaken. She had long since stopped struggling, her strength depleted and her captors' grips unyielding, their fingers bruising her pale skin. They marched her through a bewildering maze of tunnels, the path twisting and turning with such frequency that she quickly lost all sense of direction. The oppressive darkness pressed against her eyes until she began to wonder if she would ever see light again. The only constants were the weight of the darkness and the sound of her captors' breathing – steady and untroubled, as if this grim procession was nothing more than a casual stroll through familiar territory.

Her wings, normally so responsive to her emotions, hung limply behind her, the delicate membranes already beginning to dry in the stale underground air. Each step took her further from the sun-dappled forest floor, from the gentle breezes that had cradled her all her life. Down here, the air was dead, devoid of the subtle movements that kept her wings healthy and responsive. A fae without functioning wings was like a bird with clipped feathers – diminished, vulnerable, incomplete.

Occasionally, faint bioluminescent fungi provided just enough light for Maya to glimpse her surroundings, casting an eerie blue-green glow that turned the tunnel into something from a dark fairy tale – one her grandmother would never tell, but that older fae whispered around fires when they thought younglings weren't listening. What she saw in these brief illuminations did nothing to comfort her. The inside of the tree had been hollowed out and transformed into an elaborate network of passages, the wood carved with strange symbols that seemed to writhe in the dim light, as if they were alive and watching her journey with malevolent awareness. In some places, the tunnels were reinforced with what looked like bone and sinew, materials Maya couldn't identify but instinctively recoiled from. The structures reminded her of exposed ribs, as though she was travelling through the carcass of some massive, ancient beast.

The smell was the worst part – a cloying mixture of decay and something chemical that burned her nostrils with each breath. It was nothing like the rich, earthy scents of the forest floor or the sweet perfume of wildflowers that normally surrounded her. This smell spoke of things hidden away from sunlight, of processes that thrived in darkness and secrecy.

Her captors finally came into focus as they passed through a larger patch of the glowing fungi, their features illuminated in stark blue-green relief. They were fae, like her, but unlike any she had ever seen or heard described in the stories passed down through generations. Tall and powerfully built, with corded muscles visible beneath their rough-spun garments, they moved with a predator's confidence. Their wings seemed too small for flight, vestigial appendages folded tight against their backs, as if generations underground had rendered them unnecessary. Their skin had a greyish cast to it, as if they had been carved from stone rather than born of flesh and blood, with a texture like tree bark weathered by centuries of harsh conditions. Most disturbing were their eyes – pupil-less and reflective, like polished obsidian that caught and twisted what little light existed in this underground realm.

"Where are you taking me?" Maya finally managed to ask, her voice small and raw from unshed tears, the words scraping against her dry throat. The sound was foreign even to her own ears, as if the darkness had already begun to transform her.

"Quiet!" the guard on her right snapped, his fingers digging deeper into the soft flesh of her upper arm. "You'll see soon enough." His voice was like gravel underfoot, each syllable a sharp stone against her senses.

"Please," she tried again, desperation making her bold despite the warning. Her thoughts turned to those who would be missing her by now, their worry growing with each passing moment. "My family will be worried. My mother, my grandmother – they're expecting me home. They'll be searching the forest paths…"

The guard on her left let out a harsh laugh that echoed through the tunnel, bouncing off the carved walls until it seemed like a chorus of mockery surrounded her. "Hear that, Thornbark? Her family will be worried." His voice dripped with cruel amusement, like sap from a wounded tree.

"Touching," the one called Thornbark replied, his grip tightening on Maya's arm until she had to bite her lip to keep from crying out. "Perhaps they should have taught her not to stick her nose where it doesn't belong. Perhaps they should have warned her about the dangers lurking beneath the forest floor." There was something personal in his tone, as if her very existence offended him.

"But I was just..." Maya began, desperate to explain that she had meant no harm, that her intrusion had been born of compassion, not malice or unreasonable curiosity.

"I said quiet," Thornbark said with a growl, giving her a shake that rattled her teeth and sent shooting pains through her neck and shoulders. His face loomed close to hers, the fungi's glow casting deep shadows across his harsh features. "Or we'll give you something to really cry about. The King doesn't demand his guests arrive unharmed – only alive."

The implied threat hung in the stale air between them. Maya fell silent, though her mind raced with a thousand unasked questions and desperate pleas. She hadn't been doing anything wrong. She had only followed a mouse, concerned for its safety. This response was so disproportionate, so calculated, that it couldn't possibly be a simple matter of trespassing. No, something else was happening here, something she couldn't begin to understand but that filled her with a dread that went beyond the immediate fear of rough handling and imprisonment.

They descended further, the tunnel sloping downward at an angle that made Maya wonder just how deep they were going, how far below the forest floor this hidden realm extended. The air grew colder and damper with each step, a subterranean chill that seeped into her bones and made her shiver uncontrollably. Her gathering dress, woven from plant fibres designed for the warm forest canopy, provided little protection against this penetrating cold.

Strange sounds echoed through the tunnels – the distant clanging of metal on metal, muffled voices speaking in a dialect she couldn't quite grasp but that seemed related to the language of her people, and occasionally something that might have been weeping, a soft, heartbroken sound that made her stomach clench with dread. It gave her cause to wonder just how many others had been dragged down here against their will, how many had disappeared from the forest above without a trace, leaving only questions and gradually fading hope behind.

Finally, after what seemed like hours of descent, they entered a wider tunnel where actual torches burned in iron sconces along the walls. The sudden increase in light made Maya blink painfully, her eyes streaming as they adjusted after so long in near-total darkness. Through her tears, she saw a row of small, cell-like chambers carved into the walls on either side of the passage, each sealed with a crude door of interlaced roots and thorns. The roots pulsed with a subtle rhythm, as if they were still alive despite being separated from soil and sunlight. Some doors had small openings near the top, barely large enough for a face to be visible; others were completely sealed, offering no glimpse of what – or who – might be contained within.

"Home sweet home," the unnamed guard said, his tone mockingly cheerful as they stopped before one of the empty cells. He ran a gnarled finger along the edge of the door, almost caressing the thorny structure. "Not quite the forest bower you're used to, I imagine, but it'll keep you... contained."

Thornbark released her arm long enough to manipulate something on the door – a series of knots in the root system that responded to his touch like a complex lock. The root structure writhed and parted with a sound like rustling leaves, creating an opening just large enough for Maya to be shoved through. The push came suddenly, sending her stumbling forward into the dim cell. She caught herself against the far wall before she could fall completely, her palms scraping against the rough wood.

"The King will decide what to do with you," Thornbark informed her, already beginning to seal the doorway again with practiced movements of his fingers. "Until then, try to make yourself comfortable." His smile revealed teeth that had been filed to points, gleaming dully in the torchlight. "You might be here a while."

"King?" Maya repeated, confusion momentarily overriding her fear as she turned to face her captors through the narrowing gap in the door. "What king? There is no king in the forest. We have a council of elders, not a monarchy." The very concept was foreign to the forest fae, who had always governed themselves through consensus and shared wisdom.

Both guards laughed at that, the sound echoing unpleasantly in the confined space, bouncing off the wooden walls until it seemed to come from all directions at once.

"Not in your forest, perhaps," the unnamed guard said, his pupil-less eyes reflecting the torchlight like black mirrors. "The sun-dazzled fools above know nothing of the true structures of power." He leaned closer, his breath foul against her face. "But you're in King Eror's domain now, little gatherer. And he doesn't take kindly to trespassers. Especially not pretty little spies from the upper realms."

"I'm not a spy," Maya protested, the accusation so absurd it momentarily pushed aside her fear. "I told you, I was following a mouse, and I..."

"Yes, yes," Thornbark interrupted with a nonchalant wave. "Save it for the King." He made a final motion with his hand, and the root door sealed completely, the tendrils twisting together so tightly that not even a finger's width of space would remain between them. "Rest well, little spy. The King's judgment awaits."

Maya rushed forward as they turned away, pushing against the barrier with all her remaining strength, her fingers seeking any weakness in the structure. "Please! There's been a mistake!" The door held firm, the living roots responding to her touch by tightening further, tiny thorns pricking her fingers when she pressed too hard. She was trapped, as surely as if she had been sealed in stone.

Chapter Three

Alone in the dim cell, with only the faintest light filtering through minute gaps in the root door, Maya finally allowed herself to give in to the despair that had been building since her capture. She sank to the floor, her legs no longer able to support her, drawing her knees up to her chest and wrapping her arms around them as if she could physically hold herself together. Her wings drooped lifelessly behind her, the delicate membranes already showing signs of stress from the rough handling and the dry, cold air – the edges beginning to curl slightly, the iridescent shimmer dulled to a flat translucence.

The cell itself was barely large enough for her to lie down in, a wooden box carved with the same strange symbols she had noticed in the tunnels. The ceiling was unpleasantly low, pressing down from above like a living reminder of how far she was from the sky. The walls were raw wood, carved directly from the tree's interior, still exuding the faint resinous scent of living timber. In places, the wood seemed to pulse slightly, as if the tree's heartwood still lived despite the extensive hollowing. The floor was covered with a thin layer of what might have been dried moss but had long since lost any softness or comfort it might have provided.

There was nothing else – no bed, no water, not even a bucket for necessary functions. It was a space designed for punishment, not habitation – a temporary holding cell for those awaiting judgment, not a place where anyone was expected to live for any length of time.

Maya buried her face against her knees and wept silently, her tears dampening the fabric of her gathering dress, the blue-dyed plant fibres darkening with each fallen drop. She thought of her mother, who would be standing at their cottage door by now, scanning the forest edge for any sign of her daughter's return, perhaps already organising search parties with the neighbours. She thought of her grandmother, whose ancient eyes would be clouded with worry, who had always warned her about venturing too far alone but had ultimately trusted her judgment in the forest.

That trust had been misplaced. For all her knowledge of plants and small animals, for all her pride in her connection to the forest, Maya had walked willingly into a trap that a more suspicious or less compassionate person would have avoided. And for what? A mouse that had probably been bait all along, trained or coerced to lure unsuspecting targets to the entrance of this underground nightmare.

"I'm sorry," she whispered to the absent figures of her family, her words absorbed by the wooden walls. "I should have been more careful. I should have listened." The apology felt inadequate, a pebble tossed into an ocean of regret, but it was all she had to offer now.

Time passed in an indeterminate blur. Without the sun's movement to guide her, without the subtle changes in light and temperature that marked the passage of hours in the forest above, Maya could only guess at how long she had been imprisoned. It might have been minutes or hours; her body's rhythms, so attuned to the natural cycles of the world above, had been thrown into confusion by the constant dimness and unchanging cold.

Her tears eventually dried, leaving her feeling hollow and exhausted, her eyes swollen and her throat raw. Hunger gnawed at her stomach – she had eaten nothing since the morning's breakfast and the few berries shared with the treacherous mouse – but thirst was becoming the more pressing concern. Her mouth felt dry as dust, her tongue sticking to the roof of her mouth when she tried to swallow. How long could a fae survive without water? It wasn't a question she had ever needed to consider before.

She was considering trying to sleep – if only to escape her situation temporarily, to find some respite in unconsciousness – when a soft sound from the adjacent cell caught her attention, breaking through the fog of her despair.

It was a gentle tapping, rhythmic and deliberate. Three quick taps, a pause, then three more. Then silence, as if waiting for a response.

Maya hesitated, unsure if this was some new trick or torment devised by her captors. But the tapping came again, with the same pattern – three quick taps, a pause, then three more. It was too precise to be random, too persistent to ignore.

Finally, curiosity overcoming caution, she shuffled closer to the wall from which the sound emanated and returned the pattern. Three quick taps, a pause, then three more. Her knuckles rasped against the raw wood, sending tiny splinters into her soft skin, but she barely noticed the minor pain.

The tapping immediately stopped, replaced by a voice – male, low, and surprisingly gentle given their surroundings. It came through the wall clearly enough, suggesting the wood was perhaps thinner between cells than it appeared.

"You're awake. Good. I was beginning to worry they'd been too rough with you." The voice had an odd quality to it – cultured and educated, with inflections that didn't match the speech patterns of her captors. There was warmth in it, and genuine concern, both so unexpected in this place that Maya found tears springing to her eyes again.

Maya pressed herself against the wall, desperate for this connection, however tenuous. Any friendly voice was a lifeline in the darkness that threatened to drown her. "Who are you?" she whispered, fearful of drawing the guards' attention but unable to remain silent in the face of this unexpected kindness.

"My name is Hadel," the voice replied after a brief pause, as if its owner was considering how much to reveal. "And like you, I'm a guest of King Eror's hospitality." The words were carefully chosen, measured, revealing intelligence and a certain mordant wit that had somehow survived whatever ordeals this Hadel had endured.

Despite everything, despite the fear and hunger and thirst that plagued her, Maya found herself responding to the wry humour in his tone. It was a small reminder that defiance could take many forms, including the refusal to surrender one's spirit entirely to despair. "Some hospitality," she murmured, allowing a trace of her own bitter amusement to colour the words.

A soft chuckle came through the wall, the sound warming the cold cell slightly. "Indeed. The accommodations leave much to be desired, and the service is atrocious." He paused, then continued in a more serious tone. "May I ask your name, fellow prisoner? Unless you prefer to remain anonymous, which I would completely understand."

"Maya," she answered after a brief hesitation, weighing the risks of sharing even this small piece of herself. But what harm could come from a name? And perhaps names were important here, anchors to identity when everything else was stripped away. "I'm from the forest above." She added this last part without thinking, a reflexive identification with the home that now seemed impossibly distant.

"I thought as much. Your accent – it has the lightness of the upper realms." There was something in his voice when he said this, a wistfulness perhaps, or a distant memory. "The syllables dance rather than trudge. It's...

refreshing to hear." There was a pause, then: "How did they catch you, Maya from the forest above?"

She explained about the mouse, her concern for the tiny creature, and the trap that had been sprung the moment she entered the tree. As she spoke, the words tumbling out in a rush now that she had a sympathetic listener, she realised how naive she must sound to someone who clearly understood this place and its dangers far better than she did. How laughably simple the trap had been, and how easily she had walked into it.

"I feel so foolish," she concluded, fresh tears threatening as the full measure of her mistake pressed down upon her. "I should have known better. I should have been more cautious."

"No," Hadel said firmly, his voice taking on a surprising intensity that carried clearly through the wall. "You showed compassion for a creature you thought was in danger. There's no shame in that. The shame lies with those who would exploit such kindness." He paused, and when he spoke again, his voice was gentler but no less resolute. "Kindness is rare, Maya. Those who would punish it are the true aberrations."

His words were a small comfort in the overwhelming darkness of her situation, a tiny flame that pushed back against the shadows. It didn't change her circumstances, but it offered a perspective that allowed her to breathe a little easier, to feel a little less like the architect of her own misfortune. "How long have you been here, Hadel?" she asked, suddenly curious about this unexpected ally.

There was a long pause before he answered, so extended that Maya began to wonder if he had moved away from the wall or decided not to answer at all. "Longer than I care to remember," he finally said, his voice carrying the burden of accumulated time. "Time moves differently down here, you see. Without the sun and stars to mark its passage." There was a rustling sound, as if he had shifted position in his own confined space. "The guards change, the torches burn down and are replaced, meals come irregularly. But none of it forms a pattern you can trust."

Maya tried to imagine it – existing in this twilight state where one moment bled indistinguishably into the next, where seasons had no meaning and years could pass unnoticed. The thought was almost as terrifying as her immediate circumstances. "And this King Eror... what does he want? Why are people imprisoned here?" She kept her voice low, still wary of being overheard by passing guards, though the corridor had been silent since her cell door had been sealed.

Another pause, this one heavier somehow, laden with unspoken knowledge. "King Eror believes the world belongs to him – or should. The forest above, the depths below, and everything in between." Hadel's voice had dropped to barely more than a whisper, forcing Maya to press her ear harder against the wall to catch his words. "He collects things he finds valuable or interesting. Artefacts from the old world. Knowledge that others have forgotten. Sometimes fae."

A chill ran through Maya that had nothing to do with the physical cold of her cell. "Am I... a collection now?" The question emerged as little more than a breath, carrying all her fear and uncertainty.

"That depends," Hadel replied, his voice dropping even lower, as if they had reached the heart of a dangerous secret. "On how you behave when you're brought before him."

"What do you mean?" Maya shifted closer to the wall, straining to catch every syllable.

"Listen carefully, Maya," Hadel said, urgency colouring his tone, the words coming faster now. "King Eror will see you soon. When he does, you must show deference. Keep your eyes down – never meet his gaze directly – speak only when spoken to, and agree to whatever he proposes. No matter what it is."

"But…" she began, instinctive rebellion rising in her throat. The forest fae had never bowed to any authority except the natural laws of the world itself. The idea of such submission went against everything she had been taught.

"No buts," he cut her off, his whisper sharp as a knife's edge. "I've seen what happens to those who defy him. The cells below this level… they're not meant for the living, Maya." He paused, seeming to gather himself before continuing. "You seem kind, Maya. I don't want to see you broken. And he will break you, if you resist."

The word "broken" hung in the air between them, passing through the wooden barrier as though it was nothing, conjuring images Maya didn't want to contemplate. Images of wings torn and crumpled, of spirits crushed beyond recognition, of bodies altered to suit a tyrant's whim.

"What will he propose?" she asked finally, her mouth dry with fear.

"Service," Hadel replied simply, the single word falling like a stone into the silence. "All who dwell in the labyrinth serve the King in some capacity. That's the bargain – service in exchange for continued existence." A short, bitter laugh followed. "Not freedom. Never that. But existence, at least." His voice took on a more practical tone. "Given your skills as a gatherer, he'll likely put you to work collecting the fungi and roots that grow in the deeper tunnels. It's important work – they're used for food, medicine, light. The labyrinth depends on them."

"And if I refuse?" Maya couldn't help asking, though part of her already knew the answer.

Hadel's sigh was heavy with implication, a sound that carried the trauma of witnessed horrors. "Then you'll serve in other ways. Ways that leave visible scars. Or invisible ones, which are worse." There was a soft thud, as if he had pressed his palm flat against the ground. "Please, Maya. Trust me on this. Your best chance – your only chance – is to appear compliant. To bend rather than break. At least until…"

He trailed off, leaving the thought unfinished, and Maya found herself pressing closer to the wall, as if she could see through it to the face behind the voice. "Until what?"

"Until we find another way," he said after a moment, the words so quiet she almost missed them. "There is always another way, eventually. If one has the patience to wait for it."

Maya's mind rebelled at the thought of submission, at the idea of simply accepting her imprisonment and serving the being who had orchestrated her capture. Every instinct urged her to fight, to demand her freedom, to appeal to whatever justice might exist even in this dark place. But what choice did she have? She was alone in an unfamiliar realm, held captive by beings far stronger than her, with nothing but her wits – and no allies save for the unseen voice from the neighbouring cell.

"How do you know so much about this place?" she asked, still wrestling with the idea of surrender, however tactical it might be. "About the King and his expectations?"

"I've been here long enough to learn the rules," Hadel replied, a certain evasiveness entering his tone, as though he was selecting his words with particular care. "And I've seen enough to know which battles can be won and which can't. Survival first, Maya. Everything else comes after."

Before Maya could press further, a distant clanging echoed through the tunnel – heavy and rhythmic, like a slow heartbeat of metal on metal. The sound reverberated through the wooden walls, setting her teeth on edge and sending a spike of fresh fear through her chest.

"They're coming," Hadel whispered urgently, all pretence of casual conversation dropped in an instant. "Remember what I said. Compliance is survival. Show fear – that's expected – but not defiance. Never that."

"But..." Maya began, a thousand questions still unanswered, a thousand fears still unaddressed.

"Maya, please." His voice was raw with emotion now, the careful measure of his earlier speech abandoned. "If you ever want to see your family again, do as I say. We'll talk more when you return." The last words held a promise, a tiny thread of hope to cling to. When you return. Not if.

The finality in his voice silenced her further questions. The clanging grew louder, accompanied now by the heavy tread of approaching guards, the sound of multiple booted feet on the packed earth of the corridor floor. Maya scrambled away from the wall, smoothing her tattered dress with trembling hands and positioning herself in the centre of the cell as footsteps stopped outside her door.

The root structure writhed open once more, revealing Thornbark and another guard, this one even larger and grimmer, his grey skin mottled with darker patches that might have been bruises or some strange pigmentation. Both wore crude armour fashioned from what looked like beetle carapaces, the iridescent segments bound together with sinew and secured with bone pins. The effect was both primitive and disturbingly elegant, a reminder that this underground society had its own crafts and technologies, its own aesthetic that had evolved in isolation from the world above.

"On your feet," Thornbark ordered. His hand rested on a short club thrust through his belt, his fingers tapping impatiently against the polished wood. "The King has requested your presence. A great honour, for a trespasser."

Maya rose slowly, her legs trembling beneath her. Hadel's warning echoed in her mind. *Compliance is survival.* She kept her eyes downcast, her posture submissive, though everything within her screamed against such surrender.

"I am ready," she managed to say, her voice steadier than she had expected, though still barely above a whisper. "I would be honoured to meet the King." The words tasted like ash in her mouth, but she forced them out, a first small step on the path Hadel had urged her to take.

Thornbark's eyebrows rose slightly, perhaps surprised by her sudden docility. "Well, well. Already learning your place, are you?" He exchanged a glance with his companion, a silent communication that Maya couldn't interpret. "Good. The King appreciates proper respect. It makes things... easier."

As the guards seized her arms again, their grips marginally less bruising than before, she caught a glimpse of movement in the adjacent cell – a pale face pressed against a small gap in the root door, features blurred in the dim light. Hadel, she assumed. As her eyes adjusted, she made out sharp, angular features and eyes that gleamed silver in the torchlight, their colour so unusual that she wondered briefly if he was truly fae or something else entirely. For just a moment, she locked eyes with him. He gave her a single, solemn nod before disappearing from view, the silent gesture conveying both encouragement and warning.

The guards tightened their grip on her arms, urging her forward with firm, silent gestures. Maya stumbled, her feet dragging against the uneven ground as they marched her deeper into the labyrinth, her thoughts racing as she was led down narrow, twisting passages, the faint glow of bioluminescent fungi casting sickly green light on the dry floor. No words passed between her and the guards, and as they rounded another bend, Maya's heart sank. She wasn't sure if she wanted to know what awaited her at the end of this new path, but the guards' hands, unyielding and cold, made it clear she had no choice.

Chapter Four

The throne room of King Eror defied Maya's every expectation. She had imagined something cavernous and imposing, befitting a monarch who commanded such fear throughout the realm – a space that would dwarf visitors and make them feel insignificant by its sheer scale and grandeur. Instead, she was brought to a relatively small chamber, though one whose design spoke of meticulous attention to detail, with an intimacy that somehow felt even more threatening than the vast hall she had anticipated.

The room was perfectly circular, with a high, domed ceiling from which hung intricate chandeliers crafted from crystallised sap that caught and reflected the ambient light in hypnotic patterns across the walls and floor. These illuminations shifted subtly with air currents too faint for Maya to feel, creating an illusion of movement that kept her senses on constant alert. The walls were carved with scenes of conflict and conquest, fae warriors subjugating other creatures of the forest – detailed tableaux that depicted battles, hunts, and rituals of dominance. Some of the carved figures appeared to be in the midst of torment, their faces frozen in silent screams. The images made Maya's stomach churn with revulsion, and she found herself averting her gaze only to have it drawn back by some new, horrific detail.

The centre of the room drew her eyes inevitably inward despite her desire to look away. There, a massive structure loomed from the floor – not a traditional throne of carved wood or stone, but a complex nest of twisted roots and branches that formed an organic cradle. The roots, thick in some places and delicate as a spider's web in others, interwove in patterns too intricate to be natural, suggesting years – perhaps centuries – of careful cultivation. Within this tangled seat reclined a figure so still that, at first glance, Maya mistook him for a statue, an artistic representation rather than a living being.

King Eror was tall, with limbs that seemed too long and jointed in places that didn't quite align with natural anatomy. His fingers, when he occasionally moved them, bent at angles that made Maya's own joints ache in sympathy. His skin was the bleached white of wood exposed to intense cold, stretched taut over sharp features that seemed to have been carved by a sculptor with little interest in conventional beauty but an obsessive attention to the uncanny. Instead of hair, delicate tendrils like fungal growths emerged from his scalp, writhing slowly with a life of their own. They occasionally twisted together before separating again, creating ever-changing patterns that Maya found herself following despite her fear, their movement exerting an almost hypnotic pull on her attention.

His wings were enormous but malformed, the membranes torn and scarred in places, suggesting they had never been used for flight. They draped over the throne like a royal cape, occasionally twitching as if remembering their intended purpose, only to fall still again against the twisted roots. The dim light caught on the wing membranes, revealing intricate vein patterns that pulsed occasionally with a greenish fluid.

Most disturbing were his eyes – not blank and obsidian like the guards, but a vivid, unnatural green that seemed to glow from within, illuminating the hollows of his face from strange angles. There was knowledge in those eyes, ancient and cold, completely divorced from anything resembling compassion. Those eyes fixed on Maya now, studying her with an intensity that made her feel like a specimen pinned for examination, her every reaction noted and categorised.

"So this is the trespasser," King Eror said, his voice surprisingly melodic despite the harshness of his appearance, each syllable precisely enunciated with a quality that seemed designed to put listeners at ease – a deception that made his words all the more sinister. "Come closer, forest child. Let me look upon you properly."

The guards propelled Maya forward until she stood directly before the root throne, their grip increasingly painful on her upper arms, their fingertips leaving impressions that would surely become bruises. The scent of the King reached her now – not unpleasant as she might have expected, but rather like old parchment mingled with the earthy aroma of mushrooms after rain. Remembering Hadel's advice, she kept her gaze lowered, though every instinct screamed at her to watch this predator's movements, to not leave herself vulnerable by looking away.

"Do you know who I am?" the King asked, leaning forward slightly, those fungal tendrils shifting as he moved, some extending towards her as if testing the air for her scent or emotional state.

"You are King Eror," Maya replied, her voice barely above a whisper, the words seeming to stick in her throat. "Ruler of this realm."

A soft chuckle escaped him, the sound reminiscent of wind through dead leaves, devoid of true mirth yet perfectly mimicking its cadence. "This realm? My dear, I am ruler of far more than this modest labyrinth. The roots of my power extend beneath the entire forest, touching every tree, every plant, every creature that makes its home in the soil. I am the shadow that dwells beneath your sunny world, the counterbalance to its frivolous light, the necessary darkness without which no existence would have meaning."

He rose then, unfolding his elongated form until he towered over her, his movements possessing an unsettling fluidity that suggested his joints operated on different principles than those of ordinary beings. The chandeliers swayed slightly as he stood, casting moving shadows that seemed to dance in deference to their master. A single, spindly finger tilted her chin upward, forcing her to meet his gaze. The touch was cold and dry, like the caress of ancient parchment left too long in a forgotten archive, and it took every ounce of Maya's self-control not to flinch away.

"Tell me your name," he commanded, his breath carrying the faint scent of minerals and earth.

"Maya," she answered, fighting to keep her voice steady, to not betray the fear that threatened to close her throat entirely.

"Maya," he repeated, as if tasting the syllables, rolling them over his tongue like exotic fruits whose flavour he was determining. "And what brought you into my domain, Maya of the upper forest? What led you to cross the threshold that so few of your kind ever discover, let alone dare to traverse?"

She hesitated, her mind racing through potential answers, unsure whether honesty or fabrication would better serve her here. The King's eyes seemed to bore into her thoughts, as if he might pluck the truth directly from her mind regardless of what words she chose. In the end, she opted for a partial truth, hoping its foundation in reality would make it more convincing. "I followed a small creature through an opening in the tree. I was curious."

"Curious," King Eror echoed, his unnatural eyes narrowing slightly, the glow within them intensifying momentarily. "Curiosity is a dangerous trait. It leads butterflies into spiders' webs. It has been the downfall of countless beings throughout history, driving them to reach beyond their understanding and grasp what was never meant for them." His voice dropped to a silken whisper. "Yet it can also be... useful, when properly directed."

He released her chin and ambled back towards his throne, the journey taking him longer than it should have, his elongated limbs covering the distance in ways that somehow seemed to bend the space between standing and sitting. He then settled into the embrace of his seat with fluid grace, the roots seeming to shift slightly to accommodate his form more perfectly.

"You are a gatherer," he stated rather than asked, those glowing eyes travelling over her form with renewed interest. "I can smell the forest fruits on your fingers, see the way the skin is slightly stained from their juices. Even in your fear, I can see the instinctive respect for life that marks those who work with plants rather than destroy them. We have need of such skills here."

Maya remained silent, though questions burned within her. How did he know her occupation with such specificity? Had she been watched, specifically targeted? Was her encounter with the creature that led her here purely coincidental, or had it been a lure, dangled before her like bait before a trap?

"The labyrinth provides many resources," King Eror continued, gesturing vaguely towards the chamber walls with one elongated hand, the movement somehow encompassing the entirety of his underground realm. "Fungi unique to our domain, with properties found nowhere else in creation. Roots with qualities unknown to your kind, crystals that form only in the absence of sunlight over centuries. Harvesting them requires knowledge, yes, but more importantly, it requires a delicate touch, one my warriors often lack despite their many... talents."

He leaned forward again, those glowing eyes intensifying, boring into Maya with renewed focus. The fungal tendrils on his head reached farther towards her, as if trying to bridge the physical gap between them.

"You will serve as a gatherer here, Maya. You will collect what we require, when we require it, in the quantities we specify. You will learn our ways, our needs, our treasures. In return, you will be given accommodation more comfortable than a cell and the possibility – however remote – of eventual release."

The offer, presented as a magnanimous gesture befitting a generous ruler, was nothing short of enslavement, a gilded chain instead of an iron one. Yet Maya recalled Hadel's warning with crystal clarity. Compliance is survival. Resistance is suffering. The path was clear, however distasteful.

"I am honoured," she forced herself to say, shaping her features into what she hoped resembled gratitude rather than the revulsion churning within her. The words tasted like ash on her tongue, bitter and choking. "Thank you for your generosity, Your Majesty."

A thin smile stretched across King Eror's face, revealing teeth too sharp and numerous for comfort, arranged in a pattern that suggested multiple rows like those of certain deep-sea predators. The smile never reached his eyes, which remained cold and calculating. "How pleasant to encounter such good manners. They are in short supply within the labyrinth, despite my efforts to encourage them." He made a dismissive gesture towards the guards, his elongated fingers trailing faint luminescent patterns in the air. "Take her to the harvesters' quarters. She begins work at the next shift change."

The guards' hold was now marginally less painful than before, but no less controlling. They turned Maya towards the exit, the movement abrupt enough to make her wings flutter in protest.

"Oh, and Maya?" King Eror called after her, his melodic voice suddenly edged with steel, the musical quality turning discordant in a way that sent chills racing along her spine.

Dread coiled in her stomach as she looked back at him. The twisted throne seemed to embrace him more tightly now, roots shifting almost imperceptibly to cradle their master.

"Do not mistake my generosity for freedom," he said softly, each word precisely enunciated despite the quiet tone. "The labyrinth has many eyes, many ears. Some visible, others... less so. Escape attempts are... discouraged in ways I would find distasteful to demonstrate on one so new to our community."

Maya swallowed hard, her throat clicking audibly in the silence that followed his warning. "I understand, Your Majesty."

"I sincerely hope you do," he replied, those fungal tendrils writhing more vigorously now, betraying excitement at odds with his measured tone. "For your sake."

With that dismissal, Maya was marched from the throne room and back into the twisting corridors of the labyrinth. The ornate door – crafted from what appeared to be a single piece of ancient wood, its surface carved with the same disturbing imagery as the throne room walls – closed behind them with a finality that seemed to mark the definitive end of her old life.

She tried to memorise the route as they walked, to create a mental map of the passages, but they all looked so similar in the dim light that she quickly became disorientated once more. Left turn, right turn, straight passage, descending ramp, right turn again – or was it left? The uniformity of the tunnels made navigation seemingly impossible for newcomers, a design she suspected was intentional rather than coincidental.

The guards maintained their silence as they marched her through the labyrinth, responding to her tentative questions with stony indifference. Occasionally they would pass other labyrinth denizens – some fae like the guards, others creatures Maya could not immediately identify. All gave their group a wide berth, pressing themselves against the tunnel walls and lowering their eyes as the guards passed.

Eventually, they arrived at a markedly different section of the labyrinth, where the tunnels widened and the bioluminescent fungi grew more abundantly, providing improved illumination. The air here smelt different too – less stagnant, tinged with earthy aromas that reminded Maya faintly of her forest home, though with unfamiliar undertones that reinforced the strangeness of her surroundings.

Here, fae moved about with evident purpose, carrying tools and baskets of various sizes, some filled with mushrooms and roots, others with crystals or unidentifiable materials. Their expressions were uniformly grim, their shoulders hunched as if under invisible burdens. None made eye contact with Maya or the guards as they passed, though she felt sidelong glances when they thought it safe to observe the newcomer.

"These are the harvesters' quarters," Thornbark explained, gesturing with one hand to a series of small alcoves carved into the walls of a larger cavern. Each contained a simple moss pallet – noticeably thicker and likely more comfortable than the thin covering in the cell she'd been kept in before – and a small shelf for personal belongings, though few of the alcoves seemed to contain anything beyond work tools and water vessels. "You'll be assigned a collection zone and quota tomorrow. Meet them, and you'll continue to enjoy these luxurious accommodations. Fail, and it's back to the cells."

He shoved her towards an empty alcove, harder than necessary, causing her to stumble slightly before catching herself against the wall. It was cool beneath her palms, slightly damp with condensation.

"The communal washing area is down that passage," he continued, pointing to a tunnel branching off from the main cavern, from which faint sounds of splashing water could be heard. "Food is distributed twice per shift at the central cavern. Miss it, and you go hungry."

The other guard tossed a rough-spun garment onto the moss pallet. It landed with a soft sound, folding into itself like a deflated creature. "Your harvester's smock," he said. "Wear it at all times while working. It marks your station and protects your clothing from the substances you'll be handling."

With that, they turned and left, their synchronised footsteps echoing down the corridor until they faded to silence, leaving Maya alone among strangers who seemed determined to pretend she didn't exist. A few glanced her way when the guards departed, but quickly averted their gaze when she tried to meet their eyes, returning to their tasks with renewed focus.

She sank onto the pallet, clutching the smock to her chest as she surveyed her new "accommodations". The moss beneath her was surprisingly soft, yielding to her weight in a way that might actually provide decent rest, but it was still a prison, lacking any privacy or comfort beyond the basic necessity of a place to sleep. The walls were bare, lacking the carvings of the throne room, though here and there she could see faint marks where previous occupants might have scratched tallies or simple images, perhaps counting days or recording experiences now lost to time.

Exhaustion suddenly overcame her, crashing over her consciousness like a gust of wind. The day's events – from her carefree gathering in the forest to her terrifying fall into darkness, from the tiny cell to her meeting with King Eror – had drained her completely, leaving her hollow and weak. Despite her hunger and the strangeness of her surroundings, Maya found herself lying down on the moss pallet, her wings arranged carefully to avoid further damage to the delicate membranes. The material conformed to her shape, cradling her aching body in unexpected comfort.

Her last coherent thought before sleep claimed her was of Hadel. She wondered if he remained in his cell or if he too had earned "better" accommodations through compliance. Either way, she hoped she would see him again. In this dark place, so far removed from everything familiar and safe, he represented her only connection, her only potential ally. Though their acquaintance had been brief and born of mutual imprisonment, she felt drawn to his wisdom and apparent knowledge of this realm. Perhaps together, they might find a way to survive this nightmare.

Chapter Five

Days blended into one another in the perpetual twilight of the labyrinth, each indistinguishable from the last in the absence of sun or moon to mark their passing. Maya quickly learned the rhythms of her new existence – the harvesting shifts that seemed to stretch endlessly, taxing both body and spirit until exhaustion became her constant companion; the brief rest periods that never quite allowed for complete recovery, leaving her in a permanent state of fatigue; the meagre meals that left her constantly hungry, her stomach a hollow reminder of the abundance she had once taken for granted.

The work itself wasn't dissimilar to her gathering in the forest above – the careful handling of delicate growing things, the practiced movements of fingers trained to harvest without damage, the methodical filling of baskets with collected bounty – but the conditions couldn't have been more different. Instead of sunlight filtering through leaves, dappling the ground with warm, shifting patterns, she worked by the eerie glow of bioluminescent fungi that cast everything in sickly blues and greens, creating shadows that never quite settled into familiar shapes. Instead of the gentle sounds of the forest – birdsong, rustling leaves, the distant gurgle of streams – she listened to the laboured breathing of fellow harvesters, the scrape of tools against stone, and the occasional crack of a taskmaster's whip against wood – a warning that quotas must be met, that efficiency was valued above comfort, above dignity, above all else.

The air down here was different too – heavier, saturated with spores and the earthy decay of things that had never known sunlight. It had coated her lungs with each breath, making her cough until her body had reluctantly adapted to this new normal, this underground existence that ran counter to her very nature as a child of the forest canopy.

Maya was assigned to the eastern tunnels, where delicate thread-like fungi grew along the walls in intricate patterns, some resembling constellations in a night sky she could no longer see. These required careful extraction to preserve their medicinal properties – or so her supervisor, a gaunt fae named Vex, had explained. Vex's skin bore the pallor of one who had spent decades in darkness, stretched taut over sharp cheekbones and a jaw that seemed permanently clenched. His wings, unlike Maya's vibrant membranes, had atrophied to useless appendages that hung from his back like withered leaves, a sobering glimpse of what might await her after prolonged captivity.

"Hold the base firmly," Vex had instructed, his voice a rasp that seemed to scrape against her ears. "Then roll your fingers upward to collect the strands. Too much pressure and they release their toxins – useless. Too little and you leave half behind – wasteful." His bony fingers had demonstrated the technique with movements so quick they nearly blurred. "King Eror does not tolerate waste."

What these fungi were truly used for, no one would say. The question burned in Maya's mind as she harvested these luminescent threads day after day, watching as filled baskets were carried away by silent attendants to some unknown destination deeper in the labyrinth.

"You don't need to know," Vex had snapped when she'd dared to ask, his eyes narrowing to slits, his mouth twisting with contempt at her presumption. "You need only to harvest. Knowledge is a privilege you have not earned."

So Maya harvested, filling her basket with the glowing strands, trying not to think about her family above – were they searching for her? Had they given up hope? – or what purpose these strange growths might serve. Were they medicine, as Vex suggested? Poison? Components for some arcane ritual? *Compliance is survival.* Hadel's words had become her mantra, repeated silently with each fungi strand collected, each basket filled, each weary step back to her alcove at shift's end.

She watched her fellow harvesters, hoping to glean some insight from their behaviours or whispered conversations. Most were labyrinth fae like Vex, their skin ranging from alabaster white to the faintest blue-grey, their movements efficient but joyless. A few appeared to be captured creatures like herself – a diminutive sprite with gossamer wings now dulled by captivity; a bark-skinned being Maya recognised as a dryad, though withered far from its home tree; even what appeared to be a young troll, its stony hide cracked from the dry air of the tunnels.

None spoke to her beyond the most necessary communication. "Move aside." "Basket's full." "Your section ends there." Whether from fear or indifference, they maintained a distance that intensified Maya's isolation, making the labyrinth feel even more vast and inescapable.

Hadel himself remained absent from her daily routine, though she searched for him among the other workers, scanning faces during meal distributions and shift changes, hoping for a glimpse of the only being who had shown her kindness in this brutal place. She had begun to wonder if she had imagined their brief connection, if the gentle-voiced fae had been merely a product of desperation in her first frightening hours of captivity, a comforting hallucination conjured by a mind unable to accept its new reality.

On her fifth day – or what she assumed was the fifth day, given the five sleep cycles she had experienced, though time had become increasingly abstract without natural daylight to mark its passage – Maya was returning from her shift. Her arms ached from reaching into crevices for the highest quality fungi, her fingers stained a faint luminescent blue that no amount of scrubbing in the communal washing area seemed to remove. Her wings felt heavy, drooping slightly from neglect and the constant moisture of the tunnels, which weighed down the delicate membranes designed for flight in open air.

She trudged along a lesser-used corridor that she had discovered shaved precious minutes off her return journey, her mind focused on the thin gruel that would constitute her evening meal, when a hand shot out from a shadowed alcove, grasping her wrist with surprising gentleness and pulling her into the darkness. The sudden contact jolted her from exhaustion to alarm, adrenaline surging through her veins.

Her instinct was to scream, to call for help despite knowing none would likely come, but a familiar voice stopped her, the sound washing over her like cool water after thirst.

"Quiet," Hadel whispered, his silver eyes gleaming in the dim light, reflecting what little illumination seeped into their hiding place. "We don't have much time."

Relief flooded through Maya, so intense it made her knees weak and almost buckle beneath her. The emotional whiplash from fear to recognition left her momentarily speechless. "Hadel," she finally breathed, his name a talisman against the despair that had been slowly smothering her hope. "I thought... I wasn't sure if..." She struggled to articulate the doubt that had crept into her mind, the fear that he had been a temporary ally at best, or at worst, some cruel test of her loyalty to the labyrinth's regime.

"I know," he interrupted gently, his voice low but warm with understanding. "I'm sorry I couldn't come to you sooner. It wasn't safe." He glanced nervously at the main passage, eyes tracking the shadows for any sign of movement, any hint of unwelcome observers. "It's still not safe, but I had to make sure you were all right."

Now that her eyes had adjusted to the deeper shadow of the alcove, a process that happened more quickly with each passing day as her vision adapted to perpetual dimness, Maya could see him clearly. Hadel was taller than most labyrinth fae, with a lean build that suggested speed rather than brute strength. Where the guards like Thornbark were broad and imposing, Hadel was whipcord thin, built for slipping through shadows rather than commanding them. His features were sharp, almost severe, with high cheekbones and a pointed chin, but softened by eyes that held genuine concern, a rarity in this place where emotion was weakness and weakness was exploited. His wings – unlike the stunted appendages of many labyrinth dwellers – appeared fully formed, though folded tightly against his back, their colour a deep midnight blue veined with silver that matched his eyes.

"I'm surviving," Maya replied, suddenly conscious of her dishevelled appearance, the stark contrast between her current state and how she had looked in the forest above. Her dress, once vibrant with natural dyes, was now stained with fungal residue, the hem frayed where it had caught on rough wood. Her hair, normally adorned with small blossoms or leaves, hung limp and undecorated, and her wings, once her pride with their rainbow iridescence, were dulled from lack of proper grooming, the edges beginning to show signs of wear. She resisted the urge to attempt some hasty improvement to her appearance, reminding herself that vanity had no place in survival. "Thanks to your advice. The King assigned me to the harvesters."

Hadel nodded, something like pride flickering across his face, quickly replaced by his usual watchful expression. "I knew you were smart enough to play along. That's good. It gives us time."

"Time for what?" The question escaped before she could consider its implications, her curiosity – the very trait that had led her into this predicament – still irrepressible despite everything.

He hesitated, his gaze darting once more to the passage outside, scanning for threats with the habitual vigilance of prey long accustomed to predators. "Not here," he said finally, his voice dropping even lower, forcing Maya to lean closer to catch his words. "Too many ears. Some in the walls themselves." This last part was delivered with a meaningful glance at the stone surrounding them, suggesting surveillance beyond the obvious guards and taskmasters. "Meet me when the third fungi chime sounds. There's an abandoned storage area two levels down from here, just past the waterfall tunnel. I'll show you then."

Maya frowned, conflicted. Secret meetings carried obvious risks, yet the alternative – continuing this half-life of harvesting and hunger with no end in sight – seemed equally untenable. "Show me what?" Despite her gratitude for his earlier help, something about this clandestine meeting set off warning bells in her mind, caution that had been honed since her capture.

Hadel's expression softened, the wariness momentarily giving way to something more vulnerable, more genuine. He reached out to brush a strand of hair from her face, the gesture startlingly intimate in a world where touch had become associated only with restraint or guidance to work areas. His fingers were cool against her skin, but not unpleasant – a reminder that gentleness still existed. "A way out, Maya. A way back to the forest as you know it."

Her heart leapt at his words, pounding against her ribs like a caged bird suddenly sensing open sky, but caution tempered her hope, experience having taught her the steep price of naïveté. "How? The labyrinth is guarded at every junction, and I don't even know which way leads to the surface anymore. I've lost all sense of direction down here."

"I've been here longer than you," he reminded her, a shadow of old pain crossing his features, suggesting years rather than days in the darkness. "I know this place's secrets – including passages the guards don't monitor. Paths forgotten even by those who built them." He squeezed her hand gently, the pressure conveying reassurance and urgency in equal measure. "But we need to be careful. If we're caught planning an escape..." He let the sentence hang, implication enough given King Eror's veiled threats and the obvious suffering of those who had fallen from favour.

Maya studied him, searching for any sign of deception – a flicker of the eyes, a tenseness around the mouth, any of the small tells her mother had taught her to look for when trading with merchants of questionable reputation. But all she saw was earnestness, perhaps even a touch of fear – reasonable, given the risks he was taking by approaching her, by offering hope where hopelessness was the currency of control.

"Why help me?" she asked softly, the question fundamental to her decision. "You don't even know me. What do you gain by risking yourself for a stranger?" In the labyrinth, nothing came without cost – this lesson had been made abundantly clear from her first moments of captivity.

A strange expression crossed Hadel's face – vulnerability mixed with something darker, more complex, emotions layering and shifting too quickly to untangle properly. "Because no one deserves this existence," he said finally, his voice rough with suppressed feeling. "Least of all someone who entered the labyrinth out of compassion for a small creature." His hands clenched briefly at his sides, then relaxed with visible effort. "As for me, I've got my own reasons."

His answer satisfied her, aligning with her own sense of justice while acknowledging personal motives that lent credibility to his offer. Yet there was something in his tone, a note of hesitation perhaps, that lingered in her mind like a discordant note in an otherwise familiar melody.

"Third fungi chime," she confirmed, committing the details to memory, knowing there would be no written instructions, no map to follow apart from the one in her mind. "The abandoned storage area past the waterfall tunnel."

Hadel nodded, squeezing her hand once more before releasing it, the brief warmth of contact quickly fading in the perpetual chill of the underground passages. "Go now. Return to your alcove as if nothing has happened. Continue your harvesting, maintain your routine." His voice took on an urgency that emphasised the danger of their plan. "And Maya?" His expression turned grave, his silver eyes hardening to the colour of polished steel. "Trust no one else here. No matter what they say or offer. The labyrinth breeds betrayal as readily as it does fungi."

With that warning, he slipped away, moving not towards the main corridor but deeper into the shadows of the alcove, disappearing through what had appeared to be solid wall but must have contained a hidden passage. His movement was fluid and silent, displaying a stealth that spoke of long practice moving undetected through the labyrinth, another piece of evidence supporting his claimed knowledge of secret routes.

Maya stood alone in the alcove for several moments, her mind racing with new possibilities, with questions and contingencies. Hope, so long suppressed beneath the strain of captivity, flickered to life within her chest, a small flame that might be nurtured or extinguished depending on what came next. A way out. A way home. The words cycled through her mind, tempting yet terrifying in their implications. Freedom meant the sun on her wings again, the embrace of her family, the familiar sounds and scents of the forest canopy – but it also meant risk, possibly severe punishment if captured, potentially even death if King Eror's veiled threats were any indication.

Caution tempered her optimism. The labyrinth had already proven itself a place of deception, beginning with the seemingly innocent mouse that had lured her inside with its apparent distress. Could she truly trust Hadel, a stranger she had met in darkness? His kindness seemed genuine, but so too had the mouse's plight, and that had led her to captivity.

But what choice did she have? Without help, she would remain trapped in this twilight world, harvesting fungi until her wings withered completely, until her skin took on the same pallor as the native denizens, until her spirit broke under the endless servitude and she became just another hollow-eyed harvester, moving through the tunnels like a ghost of her former self.

Decision made, Maya stepped out of the alcove and continued towards her assigned quarters, careful to maintain the same downcast demeanour she had adopted since her arrival – eyes lowered, shoulders slightly hunched, movements neither too quick to suggest energy nor too slow to suggest resistance. Inside, however, her mind buzzed with anticipation and questions. How far was the journey to the surface? What dangers might they encounter along the way? Would the guards pursue them, and if so, how far? And always, circling back: Could Hadel be trusted?

She reached her alcove without incident, acknowledging her neighbours with the same minimal nods they had established as protocol, a recognition of existence without the danger of forming bonds that might be used against them. The routine felt different now, charged with secret purpose. She made a show of arranging her sleeping pallet, all while her thoughts raced ahead to the meeting to come.

Chapter Six

The third fungi chime – a resonant tone produced by striking certain hollow growths that helped mark the passage of time in the labyrinth, a poor substitute for the celestial movements that governed life above – came sooner than expected. The sound echoed through the tunnels, a deep, vibrating note that seemed to emanate from the walls themselves, resonating in Maya's chest.

Moving with deliberate casualness, she made her way towards the lower levels, using the knowledge gleaned from her harvesting routes to navigate without arousing suspicion. She passed a pair of guards at one junction, keeping her eyes appropriately lowered while her heart hammered against her ribs, certain they must hear its betraying rhythm. But they merely glanced at her –

another harvester returning from the washing area, nothing worthy of attention – and continued their conversation in low tones.

The waterfall tunnel was easy to locate – the sound of falling water carried through the otherwise quiet passageways, a persistent whisper growing louder as she approached. The tunnel itself was wider than most, its walls slick with moisture that reflected the bioluminescent fungi growing in abundance thanks to the increased humidity. The water fell from a crack in the ceiling, disappearing into a narrow chasm in the floor, its ultimate source and destination equally mysterious.

Beyond it, just as Hadel had described, was a small chamber that appeared to have once stored tools or supplies. Now it stood empty save for a few broken baskets and shelving units carved directly into the walls, abandoned for reasons unknown. Dust lay thick on the floor, disturbed only by a single set of tracks leading to the centre of the space – footprints – evidence, Maya hoped, of Hadel's earlier arrival.

He was already waiting, his lean form tense with alertness, positioned in a shadowed corner that offered a clear view of the entrance while providing concealment. He relaxed visibly when he saw her, his shoulders lowering from their vigilant hunch, the tight line of his mouth softening slightly.

"You came," he said, relief evident in his voice, as if he had been prepared for disappointment despite their agreement.

"Did you think I wouldn't?" Maya asked, closing the distance between them, her footsteps raising small clouds of dust that caught the dim light filtering in from the tunnel.

"I thought you might think better of it," he admitted, a wry smile briefly transforming his face, rendering it younger, less burdened by whatever history had shaped him in this underground realm. "Caution often overrules courage, especially here."

Doubt still lingered at the edges of her thoughts, but it was too late for second-guessing now.

"I've had this on me for a while," Hadel said, his voice dropping to a conspiratorial whisper as he carefully unrolled a crude map across the dusty floor of the storage chamber. The parchment – made from pressed fungi caps – crackled softly beneath his slender fingers. "A maintenance tunnel that the guards don't use anymore. It runs parallel to the main ventilation shafts, completely forgotten by most in the labyrinth."

Maya leaned closer, studying the drawing with intense concentration as she traced the route with a delicate fingertip. The map was detailed – remarkably so – with precise notations about guard rotations, potential hazards, and narrow passages. Small symbols marked dangerous areas, and timing estimates were scribbled in the margins with a careful hand.

"How long have you been planning this?" she asked, amazed.

A shadow crossed Hadel's face, darkening his silver eyes momentarily as though clouds had passed over twin moons. His jaw tightened almost imperceptibly. "Longer than you'd believe," he replied, the pain of unspoken years hanging heavy in his words.

Maya couldn't help but be impressed. This was clearly someone who thought ahead, who observed and calculated before acting. Clever, resourceful, and endlessly patient, Hadel was nothing like the broken, hopeless souls she had seen in the harvesters' quarters.

He indicated a series of X marks meticulously drawn along one particular tunnel, his nail tapping each one with quiet precision. "These are sensor fungi. Special varieties bred by the King's alchemists. Step on them, and they'll release spores that alert the guards immediately." His expression grew grave as he explained, "They're nearly invisible in the dim light – slightly paler, with a faint luminescent quality if you know what to look for." His finger traced an alternative path, curving away from the main route. "This way is longer, but safer. The ventilation is poor though – the air grows thin in places."

Maya absorbed his instructions, committing to memory each turn and landmark. She silently mouthed the sequence of passages to herself, creating a mental map that mirrored the one before her. "When do we leave?" she finally asked, her wings shifting slightly against her back with nervous anticipation.

"Tomorrow, during the fungi harvest. The shipment of new spores from the eastern chambers will arrive, and most of the guards will be occupied with inventory and processing." Hadel's silver eyes met hers, searching her face for any sign of hesitation or fear. "Are you certain you want to do this? If we're caught..." He left the sentence unfinished, but the implication hung in the stale air between them like a physical presence.

"I'm certain," Maya said firmly, squaring her shoulders despite the flutter of anxiety in her chest. "I need to get back to my family. They must be sick with worry by now." The thought of her mother waiting, watching the forest edge each day for her return, strengthened her resolve.

Hadel nodded, something unreadable flickering across his features – a complex emotion that vanished before she could interpret it. "Get some rest, then," he advised, rolling the map with careful precision and tucking it into a hidden pocket of his worn tunic. "We'll need all our strength. The journey isn't long by distance, but it's demanding in other ways."

As Maya turned to leave, her mind already racing with preparations and possibilities, he caught her wrist. His touch was light, almost hesitant, his fingers cool against her skin. "Maya," he said, his voice suddenly vulnerable, stripped of its usual measured control. "Thank you for trusting me."

She offered him a small smile, feeling an unexpected warmth spread through her chest at his gratitude. "You're the only one who's helped me since I arrived. The only one who's even acknowledged me as more than just another pair of harvesting hands." Her voice softened. "How could I not trust you?"

Even as she said the words, a quiet voice in the back of her mind whispered caution. Trust was dangerous here. Trust could be a trap, a carefully laid snare hidden beneath kindness. And yet... there was something in Hadel's eyes, in the way his grip had been light enough to let her pull away if she wished. He had nothing to gain by helping her – no obvious motive beyond the shared desire for freedom.

She wasn't ready to abandon her wariness completely, but for now, she would hold on to the belief that his sincerity was real. Because if she couldn't trust him, even just a little, she had no chance of escaping this place at all.

Their eyes held for a moment longer than necessary before she slipped away, disappearing down the corridor towards her sleeping quarters.

Chapter Seven

The next day crawled by with agonising slowness, each moment stretching into what felt like hours. Maya performed her harvesting duties mechanically, her fingers working the familiar patterns of plucking and sorting fungi while her mind remained fixed on the escape to come. The basket at her feet filled with luminescent caps and stems, but she barely noticed their glow or the spores that drifted lazily through the air around her.

Every guard that passed sent her heart racing, her pulse pounding in her ears as she became convinced that her intentions were somehow written across her face in glowing letters. The weight of the secret plans made her movements stiff, her responses to overseer instructions delayed by a half-second as her thoughts constantly drifted to hidden passages and sensor fungi.

When the time finally came – announced by the distant sound of commotion as the new shipment arrived – she slipped away from her work station, citing a need to use the washing facilities. The excuse was plausible; the spores often caused irritation on exposed skin if not regularly cleaned away. Instead of heading towards the communal basins, however, she made her way through a series of deliberately casual turns to their meeting point.

Hadel was waiting in the shadows, a small pack slung over his shoulder. "Ready?" he asked, no preamble necessary, his eyes already scanning the passage behind her for signs of pursuit or observation.

Maya nodded, trying to control her trembling wings, which betrayed her nervousness despite her outward calm. The translucent membranes quivered slightly, catching what little light penetrated this far into the space. "Ready," she affirmed, taking a deep breath to steady herself.

Hadel led her through a series of increasingly narrow passages, some so tight they had to turn sideways to navigate them, their shoulders scraping against the rough walls. The familiar glow of cultivated fungi diminished the further they went, replaced by natural phosphorescence from wild varieties that grew in neglected corners. The air grew staler with each turn, heavy with the scent of damp earth, decay, and something else – an ancient mustiness that spoke of places long undisturbed.

"These tunnels haven't been used in years," Hadel explained as they paused at an intersection, his voice barely above a whisper. He gestured towards a partially collapsed section ahead. "After a cave-in buried a group of workers alive in the third cycle of King Eror's reign, he sealed them off. Not out of concern for others, but because reinforcing the tunnels wasn't worth the effort – or the loss of labour."

"Comforting," Maya muttered, eyeing the crumbling ceiling with newfound wariness. A fine dust of pulverised earth drifted down as if to emphasise the precariousness of their route.

A ghost of a smile touched Hadel's lips, softening his usually solemn features. "Better the threat of collapse than the certainty of guards," he countered pragmatically.

They continued in silence after that exchange, the only sounds their careful footfalls and occasional dripping water from unseen sources. Time lost all meaning in the darkness; it could have been hours or mere minutes since they'd left the populated areas of the labyrinth. Maya's wings felt increasingly heavy against her back, the membrane drying out in the arid tunnel air. The discomfort was a constant reminder of how ill-suited she was to this underground prison, how desperately she needed to return to the moisture and light of the forest above.

"Tell me about your family," Hadel said suddenly, breaking the lengthy silence as they paused to rest in a slightly wider section of tunnel. He offered her a water skin from his pack, the gesture casual but his eyes watchful as she drank.

Maya, startled by the question after so much quiet, hesitated before answering, gathering her thoughts as she handed back the water. The cool liquid had revived her somewhat, easing the dryness in her throat. "My mother is a weaver – the best in our community," she began, her voice taking on a wistful quality. "She makes fabric from spider silk and moth wings, so light it feels like wearing clouds against your skin. Her work is sought after by fae from neighbouring forests – they bring rare seeds and crystals to trade for her creations."

Hadel gave a quiet nod, his gaze distant for a moment, as though her words had painted a picture of a world far removed from the labyrinth.

A smile touched Maya's lips at the memory of her mother's workspace, sunlight streaming through the windows to illuminate the gossamer threads stretched on the looms. "My grandmother is a healer, though she's slowing down now. Her hands shake too much for the delicate work of mixing potions, but her knowledge remains sharp. She taught me everything I know about plants and their properties, about the balance between growth and decay, healing and harm."

"And your father?" Hadel prompted, settling himself against the tunnel wall, seemingly in no hurry despite the danger of their situation.

The smile faded from Maya's face, replaced by a familiar heaviness. "He disappeared when I was young. He went on a trading expedition to the southern glades and never returned." Her voice grew quieter. "Many fae have vanished over the years, especially those who travel near the old oak groves." She glanced at Hadel, a new understanding dawning in her eyes. "I wonder now if some ended up here, in the labyrinth."

Hadel's expression tightened, the muscles in his jaw visibly tensing. "It's possible," he acknowledged, something dark and knowing in his tone. "King Eror has been expanding his domain for longer than most realise. His collectors roam far beyond the boundaries most surface dwellers recognise as dangerous."

"What about you?" Maya asked, seizing the opening to learn more about her mysterious companion. She studied his profile in the dim light – the sharp angles of his face, the unusual silver of his eyes, the paleness of his skin that spoke of a life lived away from sunlight. "Do you have family waiting for you? Someone who misses you as my mother must miss me?"

A long silence followed her question, broken only by distant water drips echoing through the passages. The sound measured out the seconds, marking time in the timeless dark.

"No," Hadel finally said, the single word carrying a weight of finality that seemed to settle in the space between them. "I have no one."

Something in his tone – a rawness, a deep resignation – prevented Maya from pressing further. The wound was clearly still open, still painful to touch. Instead, she reached across the small space that separated them and touched his arm lightly, a gesture of simple comfort. "You helped me," she said softly. "When no one else would. That means something."

Hadel stared at her hand on his arm as if it were some curious specimen he'd never encountered before, then met her gaze with an intensity that made her breath catch. Something unspoken passed between them, a current of understanding that needed no words.

"We should keep moving," he said abruptly, turning away in one fluid motion. "There's still a long way to go, and we've lingered here too long already."

The journey grew more challenging as they progressed deeper into the abandoned sections of the labyrinth. Twice they had to backtrack when passages ended unexpectedly, walls blocking their way completely. The detours cost them precious time, and Maya could sense Hadel's growing tension in the set of his shoulders and the increasing frequency with which he checked behind them.

Despite his unease, Hadel guided Maya with gentle touches and whispered warnings, steering her away from stray strands of vine that threatened to trip them, showing her how to test suspicious patches of fungi before stepping on them. His presence became a constant reassurance in the oppressive darkness, an anchor point against danger.

"Why did you stay here so long?" Maya asked during another brief rest, the question that had been building in her mind finally finding voice. They sat side by side in a small alcove. "If you knew ways out, why remain in the labyrinth? Why not escape years ago?"

Hadel's expression grew guarded, the openness that had been developing between them suddenly shuttered. "It's complicated," he said, his tone discouraging further enquiry.

"I wish I understood," Maya pressed gently but persistently, genuinely curious about this fae who had risked so much to help her.

He sighed, running a hand through his hair. "I was born here, Maya," he said finally, the admission seeming to cost him something. "In the labyrinth. It's all I've ever known."

The revelation stunned her into momentary silence. She studied him with new eyes, taking in details she'd overlooked before – the particular pallor of his skin, different from her own temporary lightening after days underground; the way he moved through the darkness with instinctive surety; his perfect adaptation to the confined spaces that made her feel increasingly claustrophobic.

"But your wings," she said at last, gesturing to the elegant structures folded against his back. Unlike the stunted, malformed wings of the labyrinth-born fae she'd seen in the harvesters' quarters, Hadel's were different. "They're fully formed, unlike the other labyrinth fae."

"My mother was from the surface," he explained, a certain tension entering his voice, his shoulders stiffening almost imperceptibly. "She was captured, like you. Brought below to serve in the King's chambers." His voice took on a harder edge. "My father was one of the King's inner circle – a high-ranking official with special privileges. My mother found ways to survive, to carve out what dignity she could in a place designed to strip it away. She protected me. She made sure to tell me everything she knew."

"She must have been incredibly resilient," said Maya. "To survive in a place like this, that's no small feat. She must have been a force." Her gaze softened as she looked at Hadel, a sense of shared understanding passing between them. "I can see where you get your strength from."

Hadel's voice softened further, taking on an almost reverent quality. "She told me stories of the forest above – of sunlight filtering through leaves, of rain falling on upturned faces, of flowers that bloomed with the seasons rather than to the artificial rhythms of the labyrinth. She named me Hadel – "freedom" in the old tongue, a language that isn't well-known around here. She was smart like that."

Maya's heart ached at the implications of his story, at the thought of a captured fae raising a child in these dark tunnels, clinging to memories of a world her son had never seen. "What happened to her?" she asked, though part of her already knew the answer wouldn't bring comfort.

"She tried to escape with me when I was very young. We almost made it to the surface." His expression darkened, a shadow of old grief passing over his features. "We were caught at the final passage – the same one I'm taking you to now. The King's punishment was... severe." He swallowed visibly. "She didn't survive it."

"I'm so sorry," Maya whispered, reaching for his hand without thinking. His fingers were cool against hers, but they didn't pull away.

"It was a long time ago," Hadel said, though his tone belied the words. Some wounds never truly healed, merely scabbed over, ready to break open at the slightest touch. "After that, I learned to be useful, to become invisible when necessary, to work the system from within. I've helped others escape over the years – those who reminded me of her."

"Like me," Maya said softly, understanding dawning.

Hadel allowed the contact of their hands for a moment longer before gently withdrawing. "We need to keep moving," he said, rising to his feet and offering her a hand up. "We're nearing the boundary zones where the old tunnels intersect with newer construction."

As they continued their journey, Maya found herself watching Hadel with new understanding, seeing beyond his stoic exterior to the complex layers beneath. His extensive knowledge of the labyrinth, his cautious nature, his determination to help her – all of it stemmed from a lifetime of surviving in this twisted realm, and from a mother's legacy of resistance that he carried within him like a flame that refused to be extinguished.

The tunnels gradually began to slope upward, a change so subtle that Maya might have missed it had she not been paying close attention. Each step seemed to require slightly less effort, as though the crushing weight of the earth above was incrementally diminishing. The air, too, seemed less stagnant, carrying faint traces of something fresher that made her nostrils flare in unconscious recognition.

"We're getting closer to the surface," Hadel confirmed, a hint of pride in his voice. "I see that your senses are good – most don't notice the change until we're much closer to the exit." He paused, raising a hand for silence as he listened intently to sounds Maya couldn't detect. "The next section is tricky – it's patrolled regularly because it's near one of the minor root entrances. We'll need to time our crossing carefully."

They emerged into a larger cavity that appeared to be a natural formation rather than something carved by the labyrinth fae. The ceiling arched high above them, lost in shadows, while crystalline stalactites hung like daggers, some so ancient they had connected with stalagmites rising from the floor to form columns. A phosphorescent fungus grew in patches along the walls, casting an eerie blue-green light that created mysterious shadows and illusory movements at the edge of vision.

"Wait here," Hadel instructed in a firm whisper. "Stay in the shadows. Don't move until I return." Without waiting for her agreement, he moved ahead to scout the path, his form quickly swallowed by the darkness as he slipped between the columns with practiced ease.

While he was gone, Maya took the opportunity to stretch her wings, which had been pressed uncomfortably against her back in the narrow tunnels. She extended them slowly, wincing at the stiffness of joints unused to confinement. The translucent membranes felt dry and brittle – a consequence of days without proper sunlight or the moisture of the forest air. Fine dust had accumulated along the delicate veins that provided structure, making them appear dull rather than luminescent. She wondered anxiously if they would still support her in flight once she reached the surface, or if she would need time to rehabilitate them.

A soft footfall alerted her to Hadel's return before she could see him. She quickly folded her wings back into place, not wanting to appear ungrateful for his guidance by bringing attention to her discomfort.

He materialised from between two columns, his expression tense but determined. "The passage ahead is clear for now, but we need to hurry," he reported, gesturing for her to follow. "The patrol will be back soon enough, and they're thorough in their inspections of this area."

They moved swiftly, keeping to the shadows, every sense alert for danger. Maya found herself holding her breath at sudden sounds – the skittering of small creatures disturbed by their passage, the occasional settling of the ancient bark.

Beyond them lay another tunnel, this one sloping more steeply upward. The walls were different here, with tree roots breaking through in places, reaching down like searching fingers. Maya could feel her spirits rising with the path – they were close, so close to freedom. The scent of soil – real soil, not the sterile growing medium of the fungi chambers – filled her nostrils, bringing with it memories of home so strong they made her eyes sting with sudden tears.

Then disaster struck.

As they rounded a bend in the tunnel, they came face to face with a labyrinth guard – not a patrol, but a single sentry who seemed as surprised to see them as they were to encounter him. He was a large fae with stunted wings and a heavily muscled build, a fungal lantern held aloft in one hand.

For a frozen moment, the three fae stared at one another, the silence broken only by the guard's startled intake of breath. Then his hand moved towards an alarm fungus growing on the wall beside him – a large orange-red specimen that would release a cloud of spores when triggered, alerting every guard in the vicinity to their presence.

Hadel reacted with shocking speed. Before Maya could process what was happening, he had launched himself at the guard, driving the larger fae back against the tunnel wall with enough force to knock the breath from his lungs. The fungal lantern fell to the ground, rolling across the uneven floor but miraculously remaining lit.

"Run!" Hadel shouted at Maya, his voice strained as he struggled to restrain the guard, whose superior size and strength were evident in the way Hadel's muscles trembled with effort. "The exit is just ahead – a root gap in the ceiling of the next chamber! You can't miss it!"

The guard managed to land a heavy blow to Hadel's ribs with a meaty fist, sending him staggering backward with a grunt of pain. Maya hesitated, hovering uncertainly, unwilling to leave her companion behind to face punishment alone.

"Go!" Hadel commanded, recovering his balance and driving his shoulder into the guard's midsection with desperate force. "I'll be right behind you! GO!"

Chapter Eight

Heart pounding, wings trembling with adrenaline, Maya forced herself to turn and sprint up the tunnel. The path twisted once more before opening into a small, roughly circular chamber. Behind her, she could hear the sounds of the struggle continuing – grunts of pain, the impact of fists against flesh, and once, a choking cry that could have come from either combatant.

The chamber walls were almost entirely composed of earth and tangled roots, creating a natural dome. And there – just as Hadel had promised – was a gap in the ceiling where massive tree roots had parted to form an irregular opening. Faint, precious light filtered through it, illuminating particles of dust dancing in the air like tiny constellations.

Maya's wings fluttered with anticipation, responding to the presence of that light even in their weakened state. Freedom was literally above her head, within reach after captivity and hopelessness.

But what about Hadel?

She turned back towards the tunnel entrance, torn between immediate escape and loyalty to the fae who had made it possible. The sounds of fighting had stopped, replaced by approaching footsteps – whether friend or foe, she couldn't yet tell.

Hadel emerged from the tunnel, blood trickling from a cut above his eye and from the corner of his mouth, his breathing laboured and one arm pressed protectively against his side where the guard had struck him. Relief flooded through Maya at the sight of him, though it was quickly tempered by concern for his injuries.

"You're still here," he said, surprise evident in his voice and expression as he took in her position near the root opening. "Why didn't you go? Every moment increases the risk."

"I couldn't leave without knowing you were safe," she replied simply, moving towards him. "Come on, we need to hurry. Is the guard...?"

"Unconscious, but not for long," Hadel assured her, glancing back over his shoulder. "I used a sleep-spore pouch – black market goods. Effective, but temporary. Others will come looking when he fails to report in."

She reached for his hand, ready to pull him towards the opening above, but Hadel remained rooted in place, his silver eyes fixed on the shaft of light penetrating the darkness. A strange expression crossed his face – intense longing mixed with something that looked almost like terror, his features caught in a battle between desire and deeply ingrained fear.

"Hadel?" Maya prompted, confusion replacing her relief as she noticed his reluctance. "What's wrong? We need to hurry."

"I..." His voice faltered, the single syllable laced with conflict. His wings, which had been folded tightly against his back throughout their journey, now trembled visibly, the translucent membranes rippling with suppressed emotion. "I can't."

"What do you mean, you can't? The guard…"

"Is unconscious, but not for long," Hadel finished for the second time, his tone firmer now, his decision apparently made despite the torment evident in his eyes. "You need to go. Now. Before others come."

Maya stared at him in disbelief, her mind struggling to process his words. "We're going together," she insisted, tightening her grip on his hand. "That was the plan. That's why we came all this way."

Hadel shook his head, gently but firmly extracting his hand from hers. He backed away from the shaft of light as if it might burn him, retreating into the familiar shadows. "I never said I was coming with you," he pointed out softly. "I said I would show you the way out. And I have."

"That's ridiculous," Maya argued, frustration building within her as precious seconds ticked away. "After everything we've been through, after all the risks you've taken – you're just going to stay here? In the labyrinth? Under King Eror's rule?"

"You don't understand," Hadel said, his voice tight with emotion that he seemed to be struggling to control. "I've spent my entire life here. The outside – your world – it's just stories to me. Legends my mother told a frightened child. I wouldn't know how to survive there, how to navigate a world without walls or ceilings."

"I'll help you," Maya insisted, reaching for him again, her heart aching at the sight of his obvious internal struggle. "My family would welcome you after what you've done for me. We could teach you – about the forest, about our ways. You could start a new life."

"No!" The force of his rejection startled her, seeming to surprise even Hadel himself. He flinched at his own vehemence, his expression softening immediately as regret replaced anger. "I'm sorry, Maya. I truly am. But I... I can't face it. The open sky, the endless space." His voice dropped to a whisper, raw with admission of weakness. "It terrifies me."

Understanding dawned on Maya like a cold wave. Hadel's entire existence had been confined to tunnels and chambers, to darkness broken only by the faint glow of fungi. The concept of an open world with no walls or ceiling, with light that shifted and changed throughout the day, would be not just foreign but genuinely frightening – a vastness beyond comprehension for someone raised in confinement.

"It doesn't have to be that way," she said gently, her earlier frustration melting into compassion. "You could adjust, with time. Many fae fear what they don't know, but learn to embrace it when given the chance."

Hadel's smile was sad, resigned, tinged with a wistfulness that spoke of dreams long deferred. "Perhaps. But not today." He glanced back towards the tunnel entrance, his posture tense with renewed vigilance. "The guard will wake soon. Others will come looking for him." His gaze returned to Maya, intense and imploring. "You need to go, Maya. Live your life in the sunlight. Be free – for both of us."

Tears blurred Maya's vision, turning the shaft of light above into a golden smear. This fae, who had risked everything to help her escape, would remain trapped in darkness by invisible bonds stronger than any physical restraint – the bonds of fear, of the familiar, of a lifetime spent adapting to captivity.

"I won't forget you," she promised, her voice breaking on the words. A tear spilled down her cheek, tracing a silvery path along her skin.

"Nor I you," Hadel replied softly, his own eyes suspiciously bright in the dim light. For a moment, he looked as if he might say more, might even reconsider. Then, with sudden urgency: "Go. Please. Don't let my sacrifice be meaningless."

A distant shout reverberated through the passages behind them – the alarm had been raised. Time had run out. The guard had been discovered, or had awakened sooner than expected.

After a final, anguished look at Hadel – memorising his face, committing to memory the fae who had given her back her freedom – Maya turned to the root opening.

Chapter Nine

Emerging from the tree was like being born anew. Maya burst into the open air, her wings catching the late afternoon sunlight and spreading wide in liberation. The sensation was overwhelming – the warmth on her skin after the perpetual chill of underground passages, the gentle breeze caressing her face like an old friend's greeting, the kaleidoscope of colours after days of darkness and muted tones that had dulled her senses to near blindness.

For several moments, she simply hovered, drinking in the sensations that had once been so commonplace, now transformed into luxuries by their absence. The forest canopy spread around her in undulating waves of green – not the sickly, phosphorescent green of fungus-lit tunnels, but the vibrant, living green of leaves drinking in sunlight. Birds called to one another from hidden perches, their songs a complex symphony compared to the oppressive silence of the labyrinth. The air even tasted different – alive with moisture and the scent of growing things, untainted by the musty decay that permeated the world below.

As the initial shock of freedom faded, grief rose to take its place, settling heavily in Maya's chest like a stone. She thought of Hadel, still below in the darkness, by his own choice yet no less trapped for it. His face appeared in her mind's eye. Tears blurred her vision once more, falling freely down her cheeks and catching the light like tiny crystals.

She allowed herself this moment of mourning – for Hadel, whose courage had outpaced his ability to embrace change; for the other prisoners, some resigned to their fate, others perhaps still nurturing desperate hopes of escape; even for the lost innocence that had led her to follow a mouse into the darkness without a thought for what might await her beyond the familiar. The enormity of these sorrows pressed against her heart, demanding acknowledgment before they would begin to ease.

Then, wiping her eyes with the back of her hand, she took stock of her surroundings, forcing herself to see the world as it was rather than through the veil of her emotions.

The ancient oak tree from which she'd emerged stood at the edge of a familiar clearing – the very place where she had been captured, where her journey into darkness had begun. Her basket still lay among the clover, undisturbed, its woven handle tilted at the same angle she remembered, as if only minutes rather than days had passed since she'd set it down to interact with the mouse.

How strange that life above had continued normally while her entire world had been upended below. The thought was both comforting and unsettling, a reminder of how insignificant a single fate could be in the grand rhythm of the forest. The sun had risen and set without pause; rain had likely fallen; animals had hunted and been hunted; flowers had opened and closed. Nature's indifference was at once humbling and reassuring.

Maya descended to retrieve her basket, her wings still feeling stiff but functional, responding to her commands with only slight hesitation. As her feet touched the soft clover, its tiny flowers brushing against her ankles, she froze, suddenly alert for any sign of danger. What if labyrinth guards patrolled the surface, looking for escapees or new captives to fill the King's ever-hungry prison? Her eyes darted to the shadows between trees, her ears strained for any sound that didn't belong to this peaceful woodland scene.

But the clearing remained peaceful. The only movement came from insects buzzing between wildflowers, their tiny bodies shimmering with purpose, and an occasional leaf dancing in the breeze, spinning lazily on its stem. No malevolent eyes watched from the undergrowth; no unnatural silence betrayed a predator's presence.

Slowly, Maya's tension eased, muscle by muscle, until she could draw a full breath without fear. She was free. Truly free. The realisation washed over her like a baptism, cleansing away the residual terror that had clung to her even as she'd ascended towards daylight.

She gathered her basket, her fingers tracing the familiar pattern of the weave, noting with mild surprise that the berries inside had dried but otherwise remained intact, their shapes shrivelled but recognisable. As she ran her fingertips over their wrinkled surfaces, a thought struck her – Hadel had probably never tasted fresh berries, plucked straight from the bush, their juices bursting sweet and tart against the tongue.

Hadel. The thought of him sent a fresh pang through her heart. Should she try to help him? Return with others from her community to free the prisoners? The thought of leading a rescue filled her with momentary purpose, a way to channel the confused emotions that swirled within her.

But the memory of King Eror's cruel eyes made her shudder, a cold ripple of fear travelling from the base of her spine to the tips of her wings. Those eyes had held no mercy, no understanding, only the cold calculation of a predator. Such an attempt would likely end in more captures, more suffering, more lives consigned to darkness. And Hadel himself had chosen to remain – not out of loyalty to the King, but out of a fear so deeply ingrained that it kept him from the very freedom she now experienced.

Some choices, Maya realised with a growing wisdom that settled around her shoulders like a new cloak, had to be respected – even when they were heartbreaking. Forcing Hadel into a world he feared would only be another kind of prison, no matter how beautiful she found it. True freedom meant choosing one's own path, even when that choice seemed incomprehensible to others.

With a final look back, memorising the labyrinth's location should she ever need to find it again, Maya spread her wings and launched herself into the air. The direction to her home was instinctive – a knowledge carried in her blood and bones that no amount of subterranean disorientation could erase. Her body remembered the way, turning slightly westward as she gained height, following the invisible thread that connected her to her family, her community, her belonging.

As she flew, the forest unfurling beneath her in a tapestry of greens and browns, Maya reflected on all that had happened – the terror of capture, the disbelief that had swiftly turned to desperation, the endless darkness of imprisonment, and the unexpected connection with Hadel. Each experience had shaped her, stripping away old certainties and replacing them with a deeper understanding.

She thought about the moment when Hadel had revealed his decision to stay behind. At first, she had felt only shock and disappointment, unable to comprehend how anyone could choose darkness over light, confinement over freedom. But now, as the distance between her and the labyrinth grew with each beat of her wings, she found her perspective shifting, expanding to accommodate complexities she hadn't considered in that moment of intense emotion.

Hadel had been born in darkness, his eyes adapted to see in gloom, his skin unfamiliar with the touch of sunlight. His whole existence had been defined by the twisted rules and hierarchies of King Eror's realm, a world where survival meant keeping one's head down and accepting the unacceptable as simply the way things were. Yet something in him – some seed of compassion planted by his mother's stories of a different world, nurtured in secret against all odds – had grown strong enough to risk everything for a stranger's freedom.

That seed had not been strong enough to overcome his own fears, to carry him across the threshold between the world he knew and the one he didn't. But did that diminish the valour of his actions? Maya didn't think so. *We can only be as brave as our wounds allow*, her grandmother often said when speaking of those who had faced trauma or loss. Hadel's courage had its limits, as did everyone's. That his courage had extended to helping her while failing to help himself made it no less real, no less worthy of honour.

The realisation settled over her like a gentle rain, softening the hard edges of her grief and disappointment. Hadel had given her a precious gift – not just freedom, but a deeper appreciation for it. For the open sky that now stretched above her, limitless in its blue expanse. For the turning seasons that would bring change and renewal rather than eternal sameness. For the simple joy of flying unhindered, feeling the air currents beneath her wings, choosing her own direction rather than being herded along predetermined paths.

As the forest passed beneath her, Maya found her tears drying in the wind, replaced by a growing sense of lightness that had nothing to do with physical weight. The burden of grief remained, a shadow that would likely never fully disappear, but it was balanced now by gratitude and a newfound clarity about what truly mattered in a life worth living.

Family. Freedom. The courage to help others, even at personal cost. These were not abstract concepts but living principles, demonstrated both in her own determination to escape and in Hadel's willingness to aid her despite his inability to follow.

In the distance, the familiar shape of her community appeared – a cluster of fae dwellings nestled among the branches of elder trees, partially hidden from ground view but clearly visible from the air. Smoke rose in thin spirals from cooking fires, curling lazily through the evening air before dissipating into invisibility. The flutter of wings indicated normal evening activities as fae moved between dwellings, gathered for meals, or returned from daily tasks.

Maya's heart swelled at the sight, expanding with emotion until she thought it might burst from her chest. Home. It had never looked so beautiful, so precious as it did now when she had feared never seeing it again. Her mother and grandmother would be there, perhaps preparing dinner from gathered plants and fruits, perhaps worried sick about her prolonged absence. The thought of their reunion brought fresh tears – happy ones this time – that blurred the approaching scene into impressionistic smudges of colour and movement.

As she approached, wiping her eyes clear with the back of her hand, Maya noticed unusual activity near the community's central gathering space – an area marked by a circular arrangement of smooth stones where councils met and celebrations were held. A large group had assembled, far more than would normally gather at this time of day, and among them she could make out her mother's distinctive azure wings, catching the light in flashes of brilliant blue. They appeared to be organising into smaller groups, gesturing towards different sections of the forest. Search parties, Maya realised with a pang of guilt and love intermingled. They were looking for her.

"Mother!" Maya called, her voice carrying on the evening breeze, thin but determined. "Grandmother! I'm here!"

Heads turned upward, faces lifted to the sky. There was a moment of stunned silence, a collective intake of breath, then joyous cries erupted like birdsong after a storm. Wings fluttered as fae rose to meet her, her mother in the lead, her azure wings beating frantically to gain height, her arms already outstretched in anticipation.

They collided in mid-air, her mother's arms wrapping around her with frantic relief, nearly pulling them both into a downward spiral before she corrected their flight. "Maya! By the seasons, where have you been? We thought... we feared..." The words dissolved into sobs, emotion too powerful for language.

"I'm alright," Maya assured her, though her voice broke on the words, betraying the lie. She wasn't alright, not entirely, not yet. But she would be, in time. "I'm home now."

More fae surrounded them, creating a protective circle of wings and concerned faces, including her grandmother. Questions poured forth – where had she been, what had happened, why hadn't she returned when expected? The voices overlapped, creating a cacophony of concern that threatened to overwhelm Maya's fragile composure.

"Let the child breathe," her grandmother commanded, her authoritative tone silencing the others despite her fragile appearance and diminutive stature. Her eyes, sharp with age and wisdom, took in Maya's fatigued state in a single glance. "Can't you see she's exhausted? Questions can wait until she's had rest and nourishment."

Indeed, the emotion and exertion had begun to take their toll on Maya's already depleted strength. The adrenaline that had carried her through her escape and flight home was fading rapidly, leaving behind an intense weariness that made even keeping aloft a challenge. Her wings drooped visibly, and the arms that had embraced her mother now clung to her for support rather than affection.

"Come," her mother said gently, shifting to better support Maya's weight against her side. "Let's get you home. You can tell us everything when you're ready, and not a moment before."

The crowd parted reluctantly, though Maya could feel their curious gazes following as her mother guided her towards their family dwelling. She caught snatches of whispered speculation, theories about her disappearance that ranged from the mundane to the fantastic, none coming close to the truth.

***

As night fell outside, bringing with it the familiar chorus of nocturnal insects and the soft glow of moonlight filtering through the woven window coverings, Maya lay in her own bed, comfortably full from the hearty meal her mother had prepared. She had recounted everything – the terror, the labyrinth, Hadel – to her mother and grandmother, watching their expressions shift between sorrow, fury, and relief. Now, wrapped in a soft blanket, she found herself surrounded by everything she had feared lost forever.

Tomorrow would bring questions. She would have to decide what to tell her community about the labyrinth, about King Eror, about the fae who remained captive below. Whether to warn of danger or protect them from fear, whether to advocate for rescue or respect the choices of those who, like Hadel, might not want saving. Decisions would need to be made, warnings issued, boundaries established to prevent further captures.

In the darkness beneath the forest, King Eror would continue his silent rule. The labyrinth might claim more unwary victims, more innocent wanderers who followed curiosity into captivity. These were battles for another day, challenges that would require strength she did not currently possess and wisdom she was only beginning to develop.

Tonight, in this moment, Maya allowed herself to simply be. To feel the softness of the mattress beneath her, to hear the night sounds of the forest and know that she was truly free, truly safe, truly home.

Epilogue

Three months passed, bringing autumn's golden touch to the forest. Maya stood at the edge of the clearing where her ordeal had begun, her wings catching the late afternoon light much as they had on that fateful day.

She had returned many times since her escape, always cautious, always alert. She had marked the ancient oak with warnings in the old fae script – symbols that told of danger below, urging forest dwellers to keep their distance. She had shared her story with the Council of Elders, who had dispatched messengers to neighbouring communities with warnings about the labyrinth's existence.

No rescue mission had been mounted. The risks were too great, the labyrinth's depths too treacherous, King Eror's power too established. This pragmatic decision had initially frustrated Maya, but with time came understanding. The forest fae were not warriors. An ill-conceived rescue attempt would only result in more captures, more suffering.

Instead, they focused on prevention – on ensuring no more of their kind would fall into the darkness below.

Maya had made her peace with this approach, though memories of Hadel still visited her dreams. In quieter moments, she wondered what had become of him after her escape. Had he been punished for his role in helping her? Or had he managed to conceal his involvement, continuing his shadow existence in the only world he had ever known?

She would never know. This, too, she had come to accept.

Today's visit to the clearing was different though. Today, she carried a small bundle wrapped in leaves and secured with spider silk. Inside lay a collection of seeds – bright berries, hardy nuts, and flower pods from plants that could grow with minimal light.

She approached the ancient oak with care, alert for any movement that might suggest a trap. But the clearing remained peaceful, bathed in the warm light of the setting sun.

At the base of the tree, where she had once followed a mouse into darkness, she knelt and began to dig a shallow trench in the rich soil. Into this furrow, she placed her seeds, covering them gently and murmuring old growth songs taught by her grandmother.

"I don't know if you'll ever find these," she said softly, addressing the silent earth and whatever might lie beneath. "I don't know if you'll ever find the courage to seek the sun. But if you do, Hadel, I want you to know that beauty grows here too, not just in stories."

It was a small gesture, perhaps a futile one. The seeds might never reach the labyrinth. Hadel might never discover them. But the act itself brought Maya comfort – a way of honouring the connection they had shared, brief though it was.

As she finished her planting, a sudden movement caught her eye. A small brown field mouse emerged from the undergrowth, its whiskers twitching as it regarded her with bright, beady eyes.

Maya went very still, memories flooding back. Was this another trap? Another lure designed by the labyrinth fae?

But the mouse showed no interest in leading her anywhere. It simply watched her for a moment, then began to nibble on a seed that had fallen from her bundle.

Slowly, carefully, Maya extended her hand, her palm flat with a few seeds offered in friendship. The mouse approached cautiously, sniffed her fingers, then gathered the seeds in its tiny paws.

"Hello, little one," Maya said softly, echoing words spoken months ago. "I think I'll call you Courage."

The mouse seemed to accept this christening, continuing its meal without concern. When it had eaten its fill, it gave Maya one final look before scurrying into the underbrush – away from the ancient oak and its hidden dangers.

Maya smiled, feeling a sense of completion wash over her. The circle that had begun with a compassionate gesture towards a small creature had closed with a similar act of kindness. But this time, she was wiser. This time, she recognised the boundaries between compassion and foolhardiness.

Rising to her feet, Maya spread her wings, now restored to their full vibrancy after months back in the sunlight. The setting sun painted them in amber hues as she launched herself skyward.

She cast one last glance at the clearing below, at the freshly turned earth beside the tree that marked the entrance to another world. Then she turned and flew towards home, her heart lighter than her wings.

The labyrinth had taught her the true value of freedom – not just physical liberty, but the freedom to choose compassion even in darkness, to find courage even in fear, to recognise love as the greatest treasure of all.

As Maya soared through the gathering dusk, she carried these lessons with her. They had been hard-won, but worthwhile. They had transformed her, as surely as seedlings transform into trees, reaching ever upward towards the light.

And in that transformation lay her true escape – not just from the labyrinth's physical confines, but from the limitations of a younger self who had yet to understand what truly mattered in this wide and wondrous world.